About the Author

Bernadette Maclean came to London from County Longford in Ireland in the 1960s to study nursing, following which she worked in a large psychiatric hospital for over thirty-five years. Prior to leaving Ireland, she worked as a bookkeeper and also had a dancing school, where she taught Irish step dancing. She was also involved in amateur dramatics, performing in such plays as 'Noreen Bawn' and 'Autumn Fire'. After she retired from nursing, she started writing songs and poetry, their popularity among her friends and family leading to her embarking on writing this, her first novel, dedicated to her late husband Iain, who found great pleasure in reading the initial drafts.

Next of Kin

First published in Great Britain in 2016 by
The Book Guild Ltd
9 Priory Business Park
Wistow Road, Kibworth
Leicestershire, LE8 0RX
Freephone: 0800 999 2982
www.bookguild.co.uk
Email: info@bookguild.co.uk
Twitter: @bookguild

Typeset in Baskerville

Printed and bound in Great Britain by
CPI Group (UK) Ltd, Croydon, CR0 4YY

ISBN 978 1 910508 92 3

British Library Cataloguing in Publication Data.
A catalogue record for this book is available from the British Library.

Next of Kin

Bernadette Maclean

Acknowledgement

I wish to dedicate this book to the memory of my late husband Iain. I would also like to offer my thanks to my daughter Lorna for her support in typing and her encouragement, without which I may never have completed the story.

Introduction

*I*t was the morning of the funeral and quite a crowd had gathered outside the village church. It was eleven o'clock on a bright summer's morning in 2011, and Luke Mulryan was about to be laid to rest. His coffin was carried into the old church by his two second cousins, Brian and Noel Finley, and two friends. Luke never married and was 83 years old when he died after a short illness. The eulogy was read by Brian Finley, who extolled Luke's virtues and his love of life with great conviction. When the hymns were sung and his favourite song 'Danny Boy' was belted out, there was hardly a dry eye in the church. There was also an air of expectancy that was almost palpable, as if some great declaration was about to be made. Luke had made a will, and rumour and gossip were rife about who would inherit his fortune, for Luke was a wealthy man and had made promises to many people. To understand this sad saga it is necessary to go back to the beginning.

Chapter 1

*L*uke Mulryan was born in the Irish Midlands in 1927. His parents, Patrick and Agnes Mulryan, owned a farm four miles from the nearest village and they regarded his birth as little short of a miracle. Being married for more than twenty years, and with Agnes now in her early forties, hope of ever having a family had long faded. It was a time in Ireland when fertility testing was unheard of, and where the local parish priest constantly visited all newly-married Catholic couples in the early years of their marriages if there was no sign of any babies being born. He usually lectured them on the meaning of the 'Holy Sacrament of marriage' and about procreation and the continuation of the spread of the Catholic faith.

Poor Agnes resorted to every remedy available to get pregnant. She listened to old wives' tales, took all kinds of potions, had Masses said and did countless Novenas, but all without result.

Patrick Mulryan blamed Agnes for failing to produce an heir and repeated continually that he needed three sons to help him run the farm. Agnes decided at one stage in the relationship that the fault was all Patrick's. She then started secretly visiting a very old woman in the village, who was supposed to be a healer and have a cure for everything, especially when her hand was crossed with silver. She told Agnes she would need to visit nine times to complete the cure and ensure a pregnancy. She gave Agnes a liquid potion to put in Patrick's tea, which was the final guarantee of a good outcome. This 'wise' old woman was nicknamed 'The Crow' by the village people.

Patrick started getting suspicious of Agnes's weekly visits to the village, as she seemed to have little or no shopping on her return. He began to imagine she had a secret lover and he had at least three likely candidates in his mind. He confided in one of his workmen, a young man called Tommy he believed he could trust, about his anxieties concerning Agnes. He asked his advice about her mysterious trips to the village. Tommy regarded himself as a ladies' man and was also a bit of a comedian not averse to playing the odd joke on his unsuspecting mates, so Patrick's choice of confidante was very suspect. He told Patrick that women of Agnes's age go through phases of wanting to explore greener pastures and it was more than likely that Agnes was looking for some excitement in her life, away from the humdrum existence of a farmer's wife, especially as the farmer never took her out anywhere. Patrick argued that Agnes was not used to going out, except to do some shopping, because even before they got married they never went anywhere apart from their Sunday walks and the odd *céilí* in a neighbouring house. There was only one public house in the village, which was called Prim. It was where most of the villagers socialised on Saturday nights, and as neither of them were drinkers, what was the point? Tommy suggested he should take Agnes to Dublin for a few nights away. They could stay in a hotel and have a meal out in a nice restaurant. He guaranteed Patrick that by the end of the first night all his worries would be over and Agnes would have fallen for him all over again.

Patrick knew he had to confront Agnes about this issue but the prospect of doing this terrified him, for Agnes had an almighty temper which matched her red hair. When he began to have trouble sleeping and could stand the torment no longer, he approached Agnes with the idea of going away together for a few days' relaxation. The shock of this proposal left Agnes speechless. She immediately imagined that it was his final bid to get her pregnant and thought a change of scenery might just do the trick.

Patrick told Agnes he would make the arrangements because he was worried she might book them into an expensive hotel. As it happened, he booked them into the cheapest hotel he could find, but promised Agnes he would make up for this shabby hotel by dining out in a posh restaurant. Everything went well and they had almost finished their meal when Patrick blurted out, 'Agnes, are you seeing another man?' She laughed so loud and for so long that they were asked to leave. She was still laughing outside the restaurant, which made Patrick think he was a fool to ever imagine Agnes looking at another man. The restaurant manager was so anxious to get them out that they didn't have to pay for their meal, which pleased Patrick enormously.

Patrick was feeling generous now, especially as the meal cost him nothing, so he invited Agnes to have a drink in a pub they were passing. He ordered a pint of Guinness for himself and a glass of gin for Agnes, and, not being used to drinking, they were both very merry after two drinks. The result of this was Patrick going on to the small stage in the pub and singing all twenty verses of 'The Old Bog Road'.

The pub landlord offered Patrick and his wife a free drink on the house on condition he did not sing again. Patrick was beginning to believe that Dublin was the best city in the world; where else could you get a free meal in a top restaurant and a free drink in a pub, all in one night?

Back on the farm, Patrick did not realise he was the main topic of conversation among his staff because Tommy had exaggerated the reason for the weekend trip to Dublin, although it was not fruitful as far as a pregnancy was concerned. In the end they both gave up hope, saying it was God's will. Patrick was content now he knew that Agnes had no interest in other men. For the Mulryans, life plodded along in its usual way, Patrick preoccupied with the farm and the farmhands and Agnes working equally hard with her housework, her vegetable garden and cooking for all who worked on the farm.

Chapter 2

*T*hen, some years later, it happened out of the blue. Agnes, now forty-six years old, was feeling very unwell, sleeping badly and could not keep her food down. Discussing her ailments with her housekeeper, Mary Ann Tuite, they both decided she was going through 'the change'. This brought about an intense hatred in Agnes towards Patrick. She believed it was entirely his fault she could not get pregnant and the thought of growing old with no-one but Patrick to look at made her very aggressive. She screamed and verbally abused him at every opportunity regardless of who was listening and occasionally threw a saucepan at him.

When Patrick could no longer stand her aggressive outbursts, he decided it would be worth the doctor's fee to find out if Agnes was suffering from some form of madness. Even the thought of putting her in a mental asylum began to appeal to him. The reason he hesitated in calling the doctor was Dr Walsh's inflated fees for a few minutes' consultation. Patrick had a reputation of being a mean, tight-fisted man.

After the doctor's visit it was confirmed that Agnes was pregnant. When the enormity of what the doctor diagnosed finally sunk in, both prospective parents walked about in a trance, laughing, crying and praying in grateful thanks for this miracle. On the 25th July, 1927, Agnes gave birth to a healthy baby boy, weighing ten pounds two ounces. He was the most beautiful baby Agnes ever saw and all the more so since he had a great head of red hair, just like her. They named their pride and joy Luke.

Baby Luke's arrival seemed to spark a change in the attitudes of all those working on the farm. It appeared to create an invisible goal, with everyone geared towards making the farm as profitable and as successful as possible. The Mulryan farm was medium in size and Patrick employed four men, or farmhands as he called them, to run it. Mary Ann Tuite had been working there since she was sixteen, starting as a housemaid. After twenty years, she had become very close to the family and Agnes now preferred to call her her 'housekeeper companion'. The village people thought Agnes suffered from delusions of grandeur and equally Agnes believed she was superior to the village riff-raff, as she called them.

Life in Ireland in the Thirties was lived under a mantle of great poverty, as the world was then in the grip of the Great Depression. The farm did not make a great profit in the Thirties and Forties but the Mulryans were nevertheless entirely self-sufficient, with a large vegetable garden and the capacity for making their own cheese and butter. They had pigs, some goats, lots of hens and a large herd of cattle, which was Patrick's domain and his pride and joy. Patrick concentrated all his time and efforts on buying and selling cattle, and believed he had made a great success of this job, even in lean times.

In his youth, Luke never noticed the poverty-stricken state of the country as he wanted for nothing. He had his own pony from an early age. He loved horses and attended gymkhanas with his father or the workmen from the farm whenever possible. He was totally spoiled by his mother, his father, the farm workers and Mary Ann Tuite. He was the only boy in primary school to own a bicycle; indeed, the only boy to own a decent pair of shoes. He was one of very few children to have a birthday party each year and going to the Mulryan farm for this occasion was a great treat for the village kids. Luke was the most popular boy in the school for this reason. Through his primary school years Luke appeared to take the lead in every school activity. He loved football and was always captain of the team. He was good at organising games and always had plans, and was usually surrounded by children. In a very short time, he developed the art of manipulation.

Chapter 3

*L*uke sailed through primary and secondary school enjoying every minute of his life. In his teenage years he rode his bicycle, which was the latest model, to the village to meet his mates. He continued to play football and afterwards hung about with the village girls.

He was eighteen when the Second World War ended and was now more than six feet tall with beautiful blue eyes and red hair – and a definite hit with the girls. It was a time of big band sounds and Luke liked dancing even more than football. He won trophies for ballroom dancing, which meant he could take his pick from the best dancers and the best-looking girls for miles around.

Agnes spent many sleepless nights worrying when Luke went out dancing. She was anxious that some shameless hussy would persuade him to run away with her. She knew what young girls were like, with their painted lips and their painted legs. She thought her Luke was the catch of the century and he had such good prospects when he inherited the farm. She believed no-one was more intelligent than Luke but she also worried that some cunning, conniving, amoral young female might trap him and he would not have the experience to resist.

Agnes was an over-protective and over-possessive mother who had her housekeeper reporting Luke's every move back to her, when he visited the village. There was no bigger gossip than Mary Ann. She made it her business to know everything about everyone and spent many happy hours relaying all she knew and heard back to Agnes.

When Luke progressed from school to agricultural college, Agnes bought him a car. The college was an hour's drive from the farm and Agnes did not want her beloved son to be a boarder there, as she couldn't bear to be away from him for any length of time. During this period Luke had many romances with the local girls but they never lasted more than a few months, which really pleased Agnes. One serious attachment had Agnes working overtime to put an end to it. Six months from the start of this affair saw Agnes hatching a plan of action with Mary Ann. She told Luke to invite the girl to Sunday dinner as she felt it was time they met. Luke went along with this without any suspicion. The girlfriend with the lovely name of Rose was presentable but still not good enough for Agnes's plans.

Dinner started well and Rose was beginning to relax, thinking Agnes was not as bad as she'd heard. Then Mary Ann stated how glad she was that she would soon be able to give up the heavy work of carrying in and peeling big sacks of potatoes for all the people working on the farm, and the back-breaking standing for hours washing and ironing for so many. She said to Rose it would be a great relief to hand this kind of work to a young woman like herself and that she was getting on now and her old arthritis was a terrible affliction. Luke sat there highly amused, knowing what was happening but enjoying it all too much to say anything. Next day he received a hand-delivered letter from Rose saying she was too young to settle down and was seriously thinking of emigrating to America.

Luke carried on playing the field with lots of different girlfriends, although Mary Ann Tuite's spying methods were often frustrated because he was able to go dancing in other counties with the comfort of his car. By now Agnes had done a little research into the estate of Lord and Lady Fitzsimmons of Kilmarick Lodge and had high hopes for Luke's future. Their large estate, which included racing stables and a stud farm, was in the next county but close to the borders of the Mulryan farm. Agnes had a plan of action to introduce the daughter, Lady Juliet Fitzsimmons, to Luke.

Agnes could imagine herself being invited to dine at Kilmarick Lodge, hobnobbing with 'a better class of people', and even dared to dream of having grandchildren with titles.

Luke had graduated from agricultural college some time ago and Agnes persuaded Patrick to hand over the running of the farm to him. Patrick did not need much persuading and was more than happy to comply with this request. He was beginning to feel tired lately and was often heard saying, 'The years are catching up with me.' Agnes had an ulterior motive for Luke being in charge of the farm. She believed it would leave him less time for the village girls and make him more appealing to Lady Juliet.

Luke loved horse racing and often went to race meetings with his cousin Noel Finley, also a keen racing fan. He already knew Lady Juliet to talk to about horses but she made no impression on him; in fact he joked with his cousin Noel that she had a real horsey look about her. This resulted in both friends having a nickname for her: Heyho Silver. Agnes would have been furious if she knew, but Luke had absolutely no interest in Juliet.

Chapter 4

*L*uke's first task in taking over the farm was to secure a number of bank loans and buy up all the land surrounding the property. His father threw up his hands in despair and begged Luke to be more cautious with money or they would lose everything. Luke took no notice of this; he had a good head for business and with the economy beginning to pick up it was the perfect time for buying and selling. He increased the cattle herd, employed a farm manager and more farm hands. His success held no bounds and this well-managed business gave him more free time for his favourite pastimes: dancing and the female sex.

The first car Agnes had bought Luke in order to keep him close had proved to be a great asset for conducting his liaisons with the ladies away from the village and the prying eyes of the housekeeper. However, this little old car had served its purpose and it was time to exchange it for the latest up-to-date model. Agnes was aware that Luke had a number of girlfriends dotted around the country and disapproved of all of them. Luke was a mammy's boy and no girl would ever be good enough for him in Agnes's eyes.

Luke worked hard and played hard until the love of

his life appeared on the scene in the glorious shape of Eileen Tierney. He had noticed this tall, beautiful girl with her amazing smile and long dark curly hair on one of his now rare visits to the village. He made inquiries about her through his cousin Noel. The only information he could get was that Eileen's family had recently moved into the area. He also heard that every young man for miles around fancied Eileen. Noel Finlay had an extrovert personality and it only took a short time before he had introduced himself to Eileen. Noel was a schoolteacher in the local primary school, who had a great interest in music. He played piano accordion in a *céili* band he managed and usually performed in the village pub most Saturday nights. He invited Eileen to pop into the pub one Saturday night to hear the band. Luke went to the village pub on three consecutive Saturday nights before Eileen turned up. Noel was on a break from playing and was able to introduce Eileen to Luke. It was love at first sight – almost like an explosion. Luke couldn't believe the feelings he had for this wonderful person, having never experienced anything like this before. He couldn't believe his luck that Eileen had fallen for him, too, and didn't give any other man a second glance.

Tom Reilly, a wealthy pig farmer, fought very hard to win Eileen's affections, showering her with expensive gifts and invitations, but she only had eyes for Luke. It was then Luke decided that the only chance of a successful outcome for himself and Eileen was to keep their relationship a secret from his mother for as long as possible. It would take time and serious planning, and maybe even marrying in secret, before his mother would accept any woman in his life.

Everything went to plan for about a year and the lovers enjoyed themselves, going to the cinema in other towns, taking long walks, visiting race meetings and occasionally going to the village pub on a Saturday night where everyone believed Eileen was Noel's girlfriend, Noel having agreed to take part in this ruse.

But by a stroke of bad luck, they were spotted by Mary Ann Tuite on a fine summer's evening, as they strolled hand in hand on their way to the cinema in a town some twenty miles away from the village. She was there because a distant relative had had an accident and had requested her help. Mary Ann thought 'What luck!' and her heart raced as she followed them at some distance. Luke happened to look back at one stage and Mary Ann, in her effort to conceal herself behind a stationary tractor, fell over, grazing her knee. In spite of her uncomfortable knee, though, Mary Ann couldn't wait to report back to Agnes. The thought of the enjoyment she would get in relaying all this news to Agnes made her feel weak with excitement.

Chapter 5

*L*uke and Eileen were oblivious to the fact that they had been seen together, holding hands, by Mary Ann Tuite, so it was a surprise to Luke to get a message from his mother stating she had to see him urgently. It was late one evening when he walked into his mother's parlour. Agnes's face was bright red and she could barely get the words out, so angry was she. Mary Ann's report about the couple was embellished with talk of the glow on both their faces and the fact that they could hardly keep their hands off each other.

Agnes had a friend who knew people in high places who could find out about the private lives of just about anybody. It was discovered that not only were the Tierneys an impoverished family but some of their relatives had led shady lives, with prison sentences for crimes of robbery with violence. Agnes worried so much about keeping up appearances and her snobbery was more to be pitied than laughed at, but social position was extremely important to her.

She immediately issued Luke with an ultimatum: that he must end the relationship with 'this Eileen person' at once or suffer the consequences of being cut out of their will. Luke argued and pleaded and tried every trick he knew to persuade his mother to change her mind but to no avail. Although Luke loved Eileen he loved himself even more, so he decided to cool things with Eileen, believing he could, in time, persuade his mother to change her mind – and he would then pick up the romance where he left off. His explanation to Eileen did not make sense, because he could not tell her that his mother would not allow her son to be seen out with someone of lower social standing, let alone marry her.

At this time Eileen discovered she was pregnant. She was far too proud to tell Luke, believing he no longer cared for her. In 1950s Ireland, being pregnant and unmarried was the most appalling situation for a girl to find herself in.

On hearing of Eileen's predicament, Tom Reilly the pig farmer lost no time in seeking to become her knight in shining armour. Eileen had remained friends with Tom since going out on one date with him, when she first arrived in the village and before she met Luke. Now after a brief courtship Tom proposed marriage and Eileen accepted, believing it was her only option. Tom was ten years older than Eileen, had his own farm, no close relatives and was considered a good catch by the standards of the time. Tom was under no illusion about Eileen's feelings for him but hoped in time she could learn to love him. Eileen had explained all about Luke to Tom but he disregarded all he heard, as being of no importance. He was overjoyed at the thought of Eileen becoming his wife.

The wedding between Tom Reilly and Eileen Tierney took place one cold November morning in 1953, in the village church. It was attended by Eileen's family, which consisted of her mother and father, four brothers and two sisters. Tom's family was that of a distant cousin and an elderly aunt. It was a quiet affair, with the wedding breakfast held in a small country hotel outside the village. Afterwards the wedding couple spent the weekend in the city of Dublin where they enjoyed a show and did some sightseeing. They spent the following week touring the west of Ireland by car. For Luke, Eileen's wedding was the worst day of his life and the one and only time he ever cried. He regretted this day for the rest of his life.

Seven months later, in June 1954, Eileen gave birth to a fine baby boy, weighing ten pounds and arriving in the world with a head of red hair. Luke was aware he had a son he could never acknowledge but still went to great extremes to find out all about his life and progress.

Eileen named her son Lucas Thomas. He developed into a bright and talented boy who excelled in all subjects in school but his greatest love was for sport, especially football. He was noticed by a Gaelic Athletic Association's official in his early teens and by the age of eighteen he was the star player for the county. Tom Reilly was so proud of Lucas and his football success and revelled in all the attention and the fact that he was treated like a hero by the village people. He never missed a match wherever Lucas was playing.

Over the years Luke and his cousin Noel Finley had become even closer friends, both enjoying football and Irish music. Noel was a bachelor who had the occasional romantic attachment but Luke didn't show a lot of interest in the opposite sex now. They both spent nearly every Saturday night in the village pub where Noel was usually playing with his *céili* band. Noel had a great personality and was usually the life and soul of any party or pub outing. Luke was happy enough with his life at this time, having accepted that Eileen was no longer a part of it. He was glad to have a friend in Noel.

The only fly in the ointment as far as Luke was concerned was having to listen to Tom Reilly's constant bragging about 'his' wonderful son, especially when Luke was within earshot. It was an open secret by now that Luke was the biological father of Lucas although Lucas seemed unaware of this, and Luke had made a promise to Eileen never to broach the subject.

Tom Reilly often went to the village pub on a Saturday night knowing Luke would be there for the sheer pleasure of winding him up, as he knew Eileen still cared for Luke. Many a night Noel had a tough time separating the two men, trying to prevent fights.

Chapter 6

The years rolled by and Luke had the odd romantic affair, which always faded out when the lady in question demanded a more permanent understanding. Luke's heart belonged to Eileen and nothing and no-one was ever going to change that. Lately he was having to spend a lot of his time at home on the farm. His father, who was now in his nineties, had been acting strangely. He refused to see a doctor and it was obvious to everyone that he was suffering from some form of dementia. He had started getting up in the middle of the night and wandering around the farm leaving gates open and then being found asleep in the hen house or the stables where he could have been kicked by the horses.

Agnes, Luke and Mary Ann Tuite were all suffering from the stress and strain of getting very little sleep as they tried to look after Patrick. At one stage the solution was to lock him in a small bedroom at night and give him a sleeping tablet crushed and disguised in whiskey. This worked for a short time and peace returned to the farm. Patrick then spent all his time sitting in the kitchen, too drowsy to go anywhere. Mary Ann complained he was always under her feet, and Agnes was finding the situation all too much because although she was only a few years younger than Patrick she was still mentally very alert. Her only problem now were the headaches which she seemed to be getting a lot lately.

In January 1976, Agnes suffered a stroke. It was fortunate Luke was at home at this time. He went to hospital with her in the ambulance and hardly left her side during the last two weeks of her life. Luke missed his mother so much and in spite of always having so many people around him, he felt very alone. He employed two male psychiatric nurses so Patrick would have twenty-four-hour care, as the housekeeper could no longer manage him and her own health was not so good now. When Patrick started having violent outbursts and injured one of the nurses, Luke reluctantly agreed to put his father in a private nursing home, where he died six months later, in July 1976. Luke's parents had died within six months of each other. Having lived long, contented lives, they were in their nineties at the time they passed away. Luke often thought how much his parents would have enjoyed having a grandson, if only things had been different.

For Eileen and Tom Reilly, life was content. Lucas had completed studying veterinary medicine in college and was looking forward to the future when a bombshell fell: Tom was diagnosed with lung cancer. His family was devastated. He had never been ill for a day in his life but he had been a heavy smoker from his early teens.

Tom had all the best treatment available in Ireland at the time and for a while it seemed to be working. When he began to feel sick again, Eileen took him on a trip to Lourdes, placing all hope in a miracle cure.

In spite of everything, though, Tom died eight months

later on 13th July, 1977, he was fifty-nine years old. Eileen was very upset at Tom's passing, as he was a kind and caring husband who had treated Lucas as his own and they had wanted for nothing. Lucas had adored him and was inconsolable. Luke and Noel attended the funeral, as did everyone from the village and surrounding areas, and were very sympathetic to Eileen and Lucas.

Luke now made the decision to sell his father's farm. It was making a healthy profit and it was a boom time for trading in land and property. He was still a relatively young man and he'd always loved horse racing, so he decided to make plans to go into the racing business. After the sale of the farm he was a wealthy man and could afford to indulge himself. It didn't take long to find the location of his dreams: a huge estate some ten miles outside the village. The house was a mansion in beautifully kept grounds. It also had a stud farm and racing stables. Luke put his heart and soul into making this venture a success. In time he developed a reputation for acquiring the best racehorses and the best jockeys and trainers in Ireland.

Everything he touched seemed to make more money, and people often remarked he was a lucky man with the golden touch. Luke did not think he was lucky, although he did enjoy life. When Luke settled into his new surroundings and had made friends with the big racing fraternity, he started to hold lavish weekend dinner parties. He always invited Noel to his parties and since he still went to football matches with him and Eileen to see Lucas play, it was inevitable that Eileen was invited too.

Luke confided in Noel after one of his parties that he planned to do everything in his power to win Eileen back and only then would his life be complete. He also told Noel he had made a will, naming him as next of kin and leaving him half his estate. The other half he was leaving to Eileen, even if he did not persuade her to marry him. He knew she would in turn leave her estate to Lucas, her only son – and his.

Chapter 7

O ver the years Luke, who was now fifty-four years old, became close friends with Eileen but their relationship remained entirely platonic. Lucas was now captain of the county football team and Eileen, Luke and Noel went to all the football matches wherever he was playing. Lucas was also a qualified vet and partner in a local veterinary practice. He had many friends from the farming community which surrounded the village, and some of these friends had been at university with him. He also had friends among the football team he played for and on Saturday nights, when he was not on call for his veterinary practice, he would meet his mates in the village pub before going to wherever the party scene was happening.

There were a few female friends among his group and one he was especially fond of was Lorna Duffy, a physiotherapist in the county hospital. They first met when he went to her clinic for treatment following a knee injury during a football match. Although Lucas liked her he was too shy to ask her out, and in any case she always behaved like one of the lads. Lorna's father owned racing stables near Dublin and also knew Luke well, being involved in the same business. It was no surprise, then, at one of Luke's splendid parties, that Lucas and his lively young friends arrived to find Lorna already there with her father and other relatives. Luke observed the way Lucas was looking at Lorna and thought what a wonderful couple they would make. He set about playing Cupid, pushing them together at every opportunity. The end of the evening saw Lucas escorting Lorna home.

Eileen loved Lorna. She was everything she would have wanted in a daughter if she had been lucky enough to have another child. Lorna was often invited to Eileen's home; they even went on shopping trips together. At one of Luke's weekend parties at Greenlawns, the name he had given to estate, it was agreed to announce their engagement. Six months later Lorna and Lucas were making wedding plans.

Luke persuaded Eileen that having a marquee in the grounds of Greenlawns for the reception would be a good idea and part of his wedding present to the happy couple. To complete his wedding gift he would pay for the honeymoon in the Caribbean island of Barbados. He wished Eileen would allow him to pay for everything but as she pointed out, 'You can't give the gossips anything more to talk about'. The wedding was a great success – even the weather was perfect – and Luke felt such pride in the son that Eileen still refused to allow him to acknowledge.

It was decided that Lucas and Lorna would live in Eileen's house, which was far too big for one person. It was an easy enough journey for Lorna to drive to work each day at the hospital and convenient to Lucas's vet practice. They all settled down happily, with Eileen very much looking forward to the grandchildren she hoped to have.

Chapter 8

Another person who attended Luke's parties whenever he was home on holidays from England was his cousin Brian and his wife Harriet. Brian was Noel's brother, but they were as different as chalk is from cheese. He had moved from the village of Prim in the Sixties to England where he'd met and married an English girl called Harriet and they'd had two children, a son and a daughter.

Brian and Harriet had been returning to Ireland on holiday every summer since the late Eighties, renting rooms in the village. Brian was a heavy gambler and as soon as he heard that Luke was in the racing business lost no time in ingratiating himself into Luke's favour. When Harriet visited Greenlawns she felt so at home there that she invited herself and Brian to spend all their holidays there; after all, Luke was their relative who was 'getting on in age' and 'must be lonely'. She told Brian: 'only people of lower status rent'. Harriet was a notorious snob with a controlling, forceful personality and more manipulative than Luke could ever be. She found out all she could about Luke's likes and dislikes with a view to making herself indispensable to him. She managed to get tickets for the best shows in Dublin as a treat for Luke and insisted he stayed at their home in London on the two occasions he travelled there to race meetings. She bought him expensive birthday and Christmas presents and spent as much time as possible in his company.

Harriet was very suspicious of Eileen. She did not appear to like her, although no-one could understand why since Eileen was an easy-going, placid person who only saw the best in everyone. Luke seemed to like Harriet, or 'Mrs H' as he liked to call her. She reminded him of his mother with her bossy, interfering and snobby ways. On one occasion when Luke suffered a bad bout of flu Harriet posted him a card with a 'Bouquet of Masses' which greatly impressed him. Although he was not a particularly religious person, he did believe in the power of prayer, something which was instilled in him by his mother in his early school days.

Harriet had discussed with Brian the situation between Luke and Eileen and drew all the wrong conclusions. She saw Eileen as a threat to what she called 'their inheritance'. All Brian's working life he had been a ganger man, or foreman, for a large construction company in London. He loved the control he held over other workmen and with a little help from his snobby wife he believed himself to be superior to most other people. He was also a bully and when he lost heavily at gambling, everyone around him felt his wrath. On his annual holidays to the village in Ireland, he loved to flash large wads of cash in an effort to impress people of his success in London.

Luke, however, was not taken in by these displays of wealth since he knew Brian bet heavily on the horses, and a lot of the time he was broke. He often borrowed money from Luke, which he never repaid, telling Harriet 'he won't even notice as he has more money than sense'. Luke was aware of this – and he also knew that Brian had been declared bankrupt some years earlier.

Luke could not understand how two brothers could be so different. Noel was his best friend and he knew he could rely on him, especially when he needed advice about people; he always trusted Noel's judgment. And Noel was the life and soul of any party. Weekend entertainment was only arranged at Greenlawns if Noel could attend with his *ceili* band.

Chapter 9

*L*uke employed a large number of staff to help run Greenlawns. The stud farm and racing stables had at least one hundred staff and the house alone had thirty staff. The housekeeper and her husband had total charge of the running of the house. They were a happy contented bunch of people, who all got along very well together. Most of the staff came from the village but slept in staff quarters except when they were off duty.

This happy atmosphere began to change when Harriet began to make regular visits to Greenlawns. She enjoyed the role of lady of the manor, a title she assumed for herself, and this was something Luke found very amusing. The smooth running of this great house began to get very rocky whenever Harriet appeared on her holidays there, holidays which became more and more frequent with every passing year. She interfered with the planning of dinner parties by changing menus at the last minute and this eventually led to the cook threatening to leave. She complained the maids were not cleaning properly and even suggested that their wages should be cut. When no one took any notice of this, she complained to the housekeeper that she had thieves among her staff as a lot of her jewellery and valuables had gone missing. When the housekeeper and her husband threatened to leave after years of loyal service, Luke had to intervene. He did not relish having to put Harriet in her place, and needed a stiff drink before he had a chat with her. The outcome was a total ban on Harriet going below stairs or having any say in the domestic arrangements of the house.

On a cold but sunny autumn morning, sitting on a seat in front of Greenlawns, admiring the structure of this great house, thinking of the wealth it conjured up and the inheritance for herself and Brian, Harriet decided she needed to use different strategies to seal their fate and secure their future. Although she knew Luke thought of himself as too old for marriage now, he was still too close to Eileen for comfort. And why was he throwing his money so freely at Eileen's son Lucas, not to mention expensive gifts for his wife Lorna? Another question she pondered was whether it could be possible that Luke intended leaving 'that awful family' something in his will. Perhaps getting on friendly terms with Eileen might be worth a try and manipulating her would be a piece of cake… or so Harriet thought.

So began a pattern of going to the races at least once a week, when Brian and Harriet were in Ireland on a long holiday. Harriet organised everything, making sure Noel and Eileen were always included. Luke was happy with these arrangements as he seldom went anywhere without Noel anyway. The plan was to make Luke believe that Eileen and Noel were in a relationship. Harriet continually remarked to Luke how close Noel and Eileen had become in recent years, and what a lovely couple they made. By now Luke had become wise to Harriet and even enjoyed her feeble little plot to make him jealous. Her real plan was to discredit the pair of them in his eyes. Luke was happy in the knowledge that Noel and Eileen would always be his close friends.

Chapter 10

Among Luke's inner circle of friends was his solicitor, Joe Maxwell. He had a wife called Barbara, two sons and a mistress and was a regular visitor to Greenlawns, loving the party scene and the shooting weekends. Luke had known Joe since he left college, where he secured a second class honours degree in law.

From an early age Joe had been addicted to gambling. When he left college he was in debt but this didn't bother him too much. Full of charm, good looks and cunning, he knew he had little to worry about.

The only solicitor in the village at this time was a man called Jim Collins, who had a daughter called Barbara, now aged twenty-five and his only child. Barbara would not win any prizes for her looks and she also had a matching dull personality. Her prospects of finding a husband were not great, although she was a good dancer and considerate in many ways.

At a local knees-up in the village hall, Joe Maxwell asked Barbara for a dance and from that moment on Barbara decided he was the one for her. Joe had no intention of having anything to do with Barbara apart from using her to promote himself into her father's law practice. Jim

Collins adored his only child and never denied her anything throughout her life, so it was inevitable that Joe Maxwell would be the future husband of Barbara Collins.

When Jim Collins offered Joe Maxwell a partnership in his law firm, it was on the condition that he marry his beloved daughter Barbara. With mounting debts and no other prospects in sight, Joe agreed.

The wedding was a grand affair with two hundred guests and no expenses spared. Barbara had the most exquisite dress and six bridesmaids. She felt she was the luckiest person on the planet and Joe felt resigned to his fate. The wedding celebrations went on late into the night but when it was time for the happy couple to leave for their honeymoon in the south of France, Joe was so drunk he had to be put to bed and the honeymoon didn't start until the following day. Needless to say, Jim Collins was not happy with Joe and warned him in no uncertain terms he would be watched closely and doing anything to upset Barbara would not be good for his health.

Joe settled down to married life. The Maxwells had two sons within the next four years. Nothing unusual happened over the next ten years apart from rows over money. Joe continued to gamble and to lose but always managed to get around Barbara to solve his problems. She would ask her father for large amounts of money on the pretext of buying expensive items for her sons. The reality was all this money went towards paying off Joe's gambling debts.

When Jim Collins retired he reluctantly left his practice to his son-in-law. He hoped Joe Maxwell would come to his senses about his gambling habits and take some guidance from his tough, strong-willed, loyal secretary of thirty years, Miss Clarke. Joe, however, lost no time in getting rid of Miss Clarke. In the end she was glad to take early retirement as she distrusted and disliked her new boss intensely.

The new secretary was a young lady called Siobhain, with whom Joe had been having a secret affair for the previous two years. Things were definitely looking up for Joe at last. Siobhain was not as gullible as Barbara; in fact she was clever, articulate and knew exactly what she wanted – which was Joe. She was also very beautiful and very ambitious.

It didn't take Siobhain long before she realised Joe's gambling was causing serious money problems. She told Joe the answer to his dilemma was right under his nose, and so began the conspiracy. Elderly clients with no known or traceable relatives, leaving their estates to charities, had their wills 'rearranged' to leave all their wealth to Joe Maxwell, who was also their executor – and witness to the will was always Siobhan. This habit became a nice little earner for this devious couple. This resulted in lots of celebrations and the odd weekend away, usually close to a race meeting. Sometimes there was a small gift for Barbara, who was oblivious to this smouldering affair.

The opportunity to use this deception did not present itself often enough for Joe to be debt free and life was sometimes a struggle, especially when trying to keep the two women in his life happy. His two sons were now away in top colleges costing a fortune in fees and although his father-in-law paid for most of this Joe was still having money worries because of his gambling. To add to this worry, Siobhain was now urging him to divorce Barbara, with just a hint of blackmail thrown into the mix. He could never antagonise Siobhain as she knew too much about his dirty dealings.

Chapter 11

The year was 2010 and it was coming up to Luke's 83rd birthday. Noel and Eileen decided they should put on something special in celebration. Although Luke suffered from arthritis in his knees and hands, it didn't stop him going to race meetings and having card games with his friends. He also had heart problems. Weekend dinner parties were less frequent these days. When Noel asked how he felt about celebrating his forthcoming birthday with a party, Luke readily agreed; in fact the thought of it really cheered him up. 'Let's make this a party to remember – after all, it might be my last,' he said to Noel.

Noel spared no effort in making it the best party ever held at Greenlawns. All the usual friends were invited, including Brian and Harriet. Joe Maxwell and his wife were also invited and Joe's dilemma now was Siobhain insisting she should come as his guest. Joe's excuse to Barbara was that he needed his secretary there, in case he had a chance to drum up some legal business.

It was indeed a night to remember. The entertainment included Noel's *ceili* band, a group of Irish step dancers, the all-Ireland champion trumpet player and a tenor of some fame. The dinner was a five-course meal and the alcohol flowed freely. Joe Maxwell felt uncomfortable knowing there were people there talking about him, some sniggering and not even lowering their voices as they laughed, saying 'wives and mistresses together are the trend these days'. This resulted in Joe getting very drunk, which was always his coping mechanism.

As the evening wore on, Siobhain began to worry when Joe started to blab confidential information about his law practice. He joked that so many people loved him that they left him their estates. He even mumbled the names of some of the clients he had defrauded. Before Barbara managed to persuade Joe it was time to leave, he let slip to Brian and Harriet that Luke had left his estate to Noel and Eileen.

It was 2a.m. before Harriet began to get over the shock and digest the news she heard from Joe Maxwell. Brian was by now far too drunk and incapable to have a conversation with her, regarding the terrible news about Luke's will. After a sleepless night Harriet couldn't face breakfast; she felt sick at the thought that they would not inherit anything from Luke after all the hard work, manipulation and persuasion she had put in over the years. There had to be some way around this terrible catastrophe. She called Brian's name and getting no reply, she stood over him in bed as he nursed an unforgiving hangover and ranted and raved, calling Luke every obscene name she could think of.

Joe Maxwell and Brian Finley had one thing in common: they were both heavy gamblers. Unlike Joe, Brian had no one and no means to fall back on when going through lean times as a result of heavy financial losses. He had long ago stopped borrowing from Luke since he was never able to repay him and Harriet thought it would be bad for their inheritance chances. Brian never admitted to losing at the races; in fact he had a lot of people believing he was a millionaire because of all the major wins he boasted he'd had over the years. But at this point in time he was broke. His creditors were demanding repayments and half the time he was in hiding from them when back home in London. Harriet was such a snob she would rather die than admit to anyone they were penniless.

By lunchtime the following day, Harriet had made a decision. They would pay a visit to Joe Maxwell; after all, they were good friends and had a lot in common, especially their love for horse racing. Joe might give them some advice about how to challenge a will and if it was possible to question Luke's mental health at the time of making his will. Harriet had looked up everything she could find on the Internet relating to law and the rights of relatives following a death. She now thought she knew everything about inheritance and even thought she could teach Joe Maxwell a thing or two about law. She had a half-formed plan in her head but would need Joe's co-operation. Getting fifty per cent of millions of euros would be a lot better than the fee Joe would get for conducting and concluding everything to do with Luke's estate.

A long discussion took place in Joe's office, with Siobhain present the entire time. Joe explained that both Noel and Eileen had been informed about the contents of Luke's will. At this point Harriet said Luke had become suspicious of Eileen and Noel's relationship and she knew he would be very disappointed if anything was going on between them since he was still in love with Eileen, even at this late stage in his life. Harriet felt a certain satisfaction in her handling of 'feeding' Luke with nasty, unfounded bits of information about a strange love affair between

Noel and Eileen. With greed and financial worries now uppermost in his mind, Joe began to see light at the end of tunnel – and fifty per cent of Luke's millions was not to be sneezed at. The outcome of this discussion was the realisation that with millions of euros at stake, something had to be done to prevent Luke's will coming to light. Luke was beginning to look frail and although he had lived a long and healthy life, he had been diagnosed with heart problems at his last consultation.

Harriet now insisted that Luke's disappointment in his lifelong friends could be reason enough for him to change his will. The decision was then made to produce a new will, making Brian Finley his next of kin and sole beneficiary. Luke's entire estate would be left to him after the usual death duties and expenses were paid. The agreement between the four plotters was that after the will was read, half of all money would go to Joe Maxwell. If any one of the four people involved talked, it would mean certain prison sentences for all, and that was all the security needed in this illegal transaction. Brian and Harriet left the solicitor office with a great sense of satisfaction, returning to England the next day full of hope and great expectations. Brian was especially relieved as some of his creditors were becoming frightening with all sorts of threats and ultimatums. He could now borrow money on the strength of his expected inheritance. Harriet was beside herself with delight at the thought of being Lord and Lady of the manor, which almost made her wish she could do something to hasten poor Luke's demise.

Siobhain and Joe celebrated their anticipated wealth with dinner in an exclusive restaurant. Siobhain made it clear to Joe that she expected nothing less than marriage now, joking about honour among thieves while issuing a few veiled threats. Joe reassured Siobhain that he would ask Barbara for a divorce as soon as possible. He also reminded Siobhain how important it was to dispose of Luke's original will in the same way she got rid of the other wills: by incineration. She promised to do so first thing the following morning. He also warned her not to get any ideas about putting pressure on him by threatening to expose their fraudulent deals. Since she had been the witness signature in all the escapades, she would suffer the same consequences as him in the event of their crimes coming to light. It was at this point that Siobhain decided not to burn Luke's original will but to hide it in case Joe needed that extra push into divorce and into marriage to her. Blackmail was an ugly way of getting a marriage proposal, but she was determined to become Mrs Joe Maxwell, regardless of the cost. She was now happy at the prospect of spending the following weekend in Paris with Joe, the love of the life.

Joe, on the other hand, was beginning to lose interest in Siobhain after ten years. The early years had been exciting and they had lots of fun together. Now he was getting bored, feeling claustrophobic and hemmed in. He was feeling more tied to her than to his wife, who gave him more freedom. There were times when he looked at Barbara and thought how patient she had always been with him and what a good job she did bringing up their two sons. In moments like this when he was feeling sorry for himself, Joe would think how unlucky he was in everything he did. All he could do now was make the most of life and perhaps a big win would solve all his problems.

Chapter 12

*B*ack in London, life was not easy for Harriet and Brian, in spite of looking forward to their future in Ireland. Keeping Brian away from the pub on Saturdays and Sundays, where he was able to put a bet on the horses, became Harriet's mission in life. She fancied herself as an expert when it came to medical matters and had worked in quite a few hospitals as a care assistant in her young days prior to her marriage, but was sacked from all of them for insubordination and trying to tell the qualified staff how to do their jobs. Nevertheless, Brian believed in her 'great knowledge' especially to do with health. He believed she had great intelligence and it was such a shame she didn't get the chance to go to university. Both Brian and Harriet had completed their school education at fourteen without any qualifications. There was only one thing she ever got wrong, Brian thought, and that was telling him he had a gambling addiction, when he knew he could quit any time he wished.

Since retirement Brian appeared to be ill a lot of the time. He suffered from high blood pressure with bouts of depression and anxiety. Harriet over-exaggerated every little sniffle or pain he had. This did nothing to improve his health but it did keep him away from the betting shop and the pub, in case he had a funny turn away from home, which he was warned could happen. Harriet had turned him into a hypochondriac and he was scared of having a heart attack without Harriet there to save him.

Brian and Harriet had two children, who were now in their forties. The older of the two, a girl called Catherine, appeared to take after her mother and had the same personality, being bossy, controlling, opinionated and very snobbish. She was married to a quiet, obedient little man called George. They had no children but they adored their two dogs. Harriet got on well with George and thought he was the perfect gentleman, who always knew his place. Brian called him a wimp and said he was definitely not good enough for his princess.

The Finley's son was called Sebastian, a name chosen by Harriet because she believed it would make him stand out from the usual common names and command the respect he would deserve, when he reached the top of his career in management and big business. Unfortunately life does not always turn out according to plan. Sebastian did not take after his father in the gambling habit, although he did have the odd bet on the horses when the two of them met on Saturdays in the pub. His addiction was women, lots of women.

Sebastian was married, with two daughters now in their twenties. His wife was a rather quiet subservient individual, who didn't seem to mind that her husband was out of town every weekend without her. He had numerous love affairs, some short term and some of long duration but always with girls young enough to be his daughters. Relatives and friends debated whether it was an open marriage, while others suggested they stayed together for financial reasons. Harriet and Brian know nothing about Sebastian's extramarital affairs but would not have believed it of their golden boy in any case.

Then it happened… Sebastian turned up at his mother's home carrying two suitcases. He was in a very angry mood, saying his wife had packed his cases and left them outside his house. She even had the locks changed while he was 'away on business' for the weekend. It appeared an anonymous letter was posted to his wife by some busybody telling some 'fabricated story and lies about an affair' he was supposed to be having. He was not even given a chance to explain and all because someone was jealous and wanted to cause trouble. He believed it was someone who fancied him. He always had a very high opinion of himself.

Harriet's first reaction on seeing Sebastian standing there looking so dejected and carrying two battered looking suitcases, was to worry about what the neighbours would think. She grabbed him by the shoulders before he could say any more, pulled him into her hall, then looked up and down the road, hoping no one had seen him. Keeping up appearances was very important to her. She was always boasting about Sebastian's success and the happy family man he was to anyone who would listen to her.

Fate now seemed to play a part and stepped in to stem their embarrassment in the form of a letter from Ireland. Noel had written to say Luke was in hospital and although his condition was not considered to be serious, he thought he had better let them know. Harriet immediately booked two flights to Ireland. She made a point of informing her neighbours that she had requested her son stay at their house while they were in Ireland, as she didn't want 'the worry of their house being burgled with so many valuables in it' while they were away looking after a sick relative. The neighbours were more than happy to see the back of Harriet, even for a short time. She had no idea how uncomfortable she made them feel.

Chapter 13

*P*rior to his admission to hospital, life at Greenlawns continued to be enjoyable and relaxing for Luke. He didn't go out much these days but really enjoyed it when Eileen brought her grandsons round to visit him. Lucas and Lorna had twin boys, who thoroughly enjoyed visiting the 'old man'. They were now in their late teens and were both studying veterinary medicine in college and following in their father's footsteps. They loved horses and never tired of talking to Luke about the horses he bred and the races his horses won. They both had a keen interest in show jumping. Luke believed it was in their blood.

During one of these visits Eileen thought Luke was looking a little bit under the weather. He was more quiet than usual and was coughing a lot, and when he told Eileen he was having some chest pains, she called his doctor immediately. She also called Noel. The doctor decided to send him to hospital, although he was not unduly concerned, taking Luke's age into consideration, but at eighty-three it was better not to take any chances. Noel accompanied him in the ambulance.

All the usual tests were carried out in the first few days after admission. Eileen and Noel visited every day, which helped to cheer Luke up. At the end of the week he appeared to be on the road to recovery but after a few days at home, everything suddenly changed. Noel got a call in the middle of the night saying Luke had collapsed and had been rushed to hospital. Noel got there just in time to hold Luke's hand during the last minutes of his life. His last words to Noel were: 'You were always there for me, so make sure you enjoy the money and give Eileen my love.'

By the time Brian and Harriet arrived from London, Luke was already dead. They went straight to Greenlawns – after all, they believed, it would soon belong to them. The funeral arrangements had all been taken care of long before Luke got sick, as he didn't believe in leaving anything to chance but in order and tidiness. Brian and Harriet behaved like the chief mourners. They sat in the front row of the church close to the coffin and when Noel informed them he was next of kin they didn't bat an eyelid. Harriet shed copious amounts of tears at the burial; in fact she had to be held up by Brian at one stage.

Watching this display of grief, with some amusement, was Siobhain, who was there at the funeral with Joe Maxwell and his wife. 'I bet they are tears of joy and expectation,' she thought.

The reading of Luke's will in his solicitors' office some weeks after the funeral was the next major event in the village. Luke had told most of his staff at Greenlawns that he would not forget them when he died. He'd also made promises to a number of associates in and around the village. The whole village was shocked at the revelation that this wasn't so – and none more so than Noel and Eileen.

Harriet had by now firmly installed herself at

Greenlawns as lady of the manor. She sacked half the domestic staff who had given her backchat in the past and made life so unbearable for the rest of the staff, that within a short time she had recruited an almost completely new crew. The housekeeper and her husband were still there but seriously considering early retirement.

About this time, Harriet wanted to have a party at Greenlawns to celebrate their good fortune but was advised by Joe Maxwell that it would be seen by many to be in poor taste, so soon after Luke's death, not to mention the disappointment so many people felt after the reading of the will.

She opted for a small tea party instead, for just herself, Brian, Joe Maxwell and his wife. She told Joe there was no need to bring his secretary, for she considered Siobhain to be a 'mere secretary' and a little beneath them in their now exalted status. Barbara Maxwell was not aware of the conspiracy involving Luke's will. She had assumed her husband had earned a vast cheque for his job in conducting and concluding Luke's affairs.

During the tea party Harriet managed to persuade her guests that all four of them should enjoy a break with a holiday in the sun, as part of their celebrations. She took it on herself to book flights, arrange accommodation and other details for two weeks in the Bahamas. Again secrecy was important as they didn't want to rub people's noses in their good fortune, as quite a few people had expected something in Luke's will.

Joe Maxwell did not want Siobhain to know anything about this forthcoming trip. He also felt he could do with a break away from her. Next day, in his office, he told her he was going to a London hospital for surgery on his foot. He had, in the past, visited a Harley Street surgeon regarding a long-standing problem with his left foot, so he knew she would believe him. He explained he would be in hospital for a few days but would recuperate at his wife's cousin's place, as she happened to have a house near the hospital. This was the main reason his wife would accompany him, to visit her cousin and enjoy her greatest passion: shopping. He promised Siobhain he would be back in two weeks and arrange a surprise present for her then. Siobhain was delighted, believing she would soon be making wedding plans for herself and Joe.

Chapter 14

*T*he Bahamas was the most perfect place for this dubious foursome to indulge themselves and celebrate their good luck. Everything went so well, from their taxi to the airport to the most enjoyable flight, and Harriet knew she had outdone herself in choosing this destination. It was a five-star hotel, close to a wonderful beach, and the taxi service there was second to none.

Harriet believed she had a lot in common with Barbara Maxwell. They both had a love for shopping for fashion and antiques and they both loved the pampering sessions in the hotel spa. Joe and Brian were also in their element after discovering a casino quite near the hotel. For these two gamblers, this holiday was a dream come true.

Joe and Brian became close friends during this trip, and managed to arrange their days with such precision that they had lots of time for the casino. In order to prevent the ladies (especially Harriet) from organising their time schedule, the two gentlemen wined and dined their spouses, took them sailing and to shows and cabarets. They arranged to have chocolates, roses and even orchids sent with elaborate cards to each hotel suite at various intervals, and still had time for their favourite hobby. Harriet adored this display of wealth as it made her feel so superior and so in control.

This wonderful holiday passed so quickly and soon they were on their way back to the airport. Harriet and Barbara felt so good and were so laden down with presents that nothing could dampen their spirits. It was a different story for Joe and Brian. Both men won considerable amounts of cash in the casino during the first week, but in the second week their luck had run out. Having spent so much time and money there, they'd lost all they won and more. They were now walking behind the ladies and quietly talking about how soon they could sell Greenlawns.

Joe phoned his secretary Siobhain every second day while he was in the Bahamas. He made sure he checked the London weather forecast before he made these calls, as he couldn't take a chance on her finding out where he really was. They chatted about the weather and Joe gave her details about his foot operation and the progress he was making. He constantly declared his love for her and how much he missed her. During his last call, Joe said how much he was looking forward to being with her again and the great surprise he had planned for her.

Chapter 15

While playing rugby for his college, Joe Maxwell's son John sustained an injury to his wrist, which entitled him to a few days away from his studies. The injury was a minor sprain to his left wrist and John saw it as a great opportunity to have a few days at home. His parents were away in the Bahamas and he could take advantage of the empty house to have a real party with his friends and some village mates. He had just one thing to do before leaving college. He must telephone his dad's secretary and find out the exact time his parents were due back. No point in making the journey home if his parents were going to walk in during one of his noisy parties. They were always so disapproving.

It was a lovely Thursday morning when Siobhain took the call from John Maxwell enquiring what time his parents were due back from the Bahamas. When she tried to explain that his parents were in London, where his dad was recovering from foot surgery, John did not at first grasp the significance of her insistence that his parents were in London, and even ventured to add he had received several postcards from his mum in the Bahamas and that their friends, the Finleys, were on holidays there with them.

John was aware of his father's womanising and various affairs. He knew about Siobhain's long affair with his father, as did most of the village people, but he didn't care what his parents got up to as long as he was getting his allowance. He was a real chip off the old block and as long as he was enjoying life he would never rock the boat. When he finally realised his father had kept Siobhain in the dark about his trip to the Bahamas he knew there had to be a reason. At this point he tried to backtrack, saying late nights studying and exams had got him confused and all he wanted to know was the time they were due back.

Suspicion grew in Siobhain's mind and she decided that a little checking might be worth the effort. She contacted Dublin airport information desk, saying she needed to know the time of arrival of Joe Maxwell's flight, due in on Saturday, as his son had been involved in an accident. She also stated she was a relative and the situation was urgent. After some hesitation, Siobhain was given all the information she needed. It was bad enough that Joe had lied to her so elaborately but to add insult to injury he had gone away with the other co-conspirators: Brian Finley and his awful wife.

Siobhain was furious and set about getting her revenge with all the energy she could muster. She realised now that Joe never had any intention of leaving his wife; after all, she had been asking him for nearly ten years. She couldn't believe he would take a chance on her spilling the beans on all the crooked deals they were involved in, but of course he believed she could never talk without incriminating herself. Right now, though, she was prepared to go to prison and nothing would stop her talking. It was a stroke of luck that she had not got round to destroying Luke Mulryan's original will, as she had done with the other wills, on Joe Maxwell's instructions.

Siobhain went to the *garda* station immediately. She told the station officer, she wished to speak to someone about a number of serious frauds. She then spoke to two detectives from the serious crime squad for two hours. She produced Luke Mulryan's original will and the forged will, with her witness signature. She was warned she faced prison for her part in these crimes but if she co-operated with the authorities and became witness for the prosecution she might receive a lighter sentence. In the intervening time, she was released on police bail, pending further investigation.

Chapter 16

Saturday afternoon is usually a busy time at Dublin airport but on this particular day there was hardly space to move. Apart from the travelling public and friends, there were so many reporters and photographers that it looked as if a celebrity or pop star was expected imminently. It appeared someone had leaked the news of an expected arrest to do with a major crime. With the number of police cars surrounding the airport, it looked like something big was about to happen.

When Joe and Barbara Maxwell with Brian and Harriet Finley finally got their luggage off the carousel and breezed through the automatic doors of the airport, looking beautifully tanned and carefree, they were immediately surrounded by *gardai* and plain clothes detectives. They acknowledged their identification and were then read their rights and informed they were under arrest on suspicion of fraud. Harriet shouted it was a case of mistaken identity and demanded an apology – and when this request was ignored she stated she knew the law and with friends in high places, she would see them all sacked. Brian and Joe remained silent and Barbara just looked bewildered. All four were handcuffed, as the photographers' cameras flashed furiously. They were then driven away in separate police cars.

The following morning, total shock and disbelief was clearly showing on the faces of the accused in the newspapers. In the crowd that was watching the scene at the airport, one man was overheard by Harriet saying, 'I heard it was all to do with a next-of-kin inheritance issue,' to which his friend replied, with a smirk on his face, 'They should have gone to Knock (N.O.K.) airport!' Harriet then said in a croaking voice, 'Such uncivilised people'. All this was duly reported along with photographs in the daily newspapers the next day.

At the *garda* station the Maxwells and Finleys were given time to arrange for their solicitors to come and represent them. Interviews went on well into the night. At 2a.m., Barbara Maxwell was released, after investigators were convinced and had established that she knew nothing about any conspiracy or fraud being perpetrated. After spending the night in custody, the remaining three accused attended a court hearing at 11a.m. They were formally charged with fraud and conspiracy to pervert the course of justice. Joe Maxwell was granted bail set at 30,000 euros. Brian and Harriet Finley's bail was set at 20,000 euros each and they were ordered not to return to Greenlawns, which was now in the hands of the courts. They were also ordered not to leave the country.

Harriet was now blaming Brian's gambling for everything. To have to eat humble pie and rent rooms in the village again was the last straw. They tried to avoid people by keeping themselves to themselves but Brian still managed to carry on with his gambling by telephone betting. Harriet became depressed; their fall from such high status was almost too much to bear. Since their bail conditions did not allow them to return home to England, Harriet was hopeful that her friends and neighbours there would not have heard about their dilemma and the shame of it.

The village gossips had a field day, going over with great delight all the details of the arrests at the airport. They were also enraged by what was done by such snobbish people to Noel and Eileen. Their favourite saying was, 'Oh, how the mighty have fallen'. All Harriet and Brian could do now was keep a low profile until their case came to court, when hopefully they would be able to return to England and not go to prison.

Joe Maxwell could not practise law while under investigation, and so he was now out of work, but still gambling and hoping for that elusive big win. The fact that Barbara had not thrown him out meant he had at least a roof over his head, and Barbara's own money kept the family afloat. Siobhain had by now moved out of the village and no-one knew where she was. Joe had tried, without success, to find her. He was desperate to meet her now, as he knew how hot-headed and vindictive she could be. Joe and the Finleys had not been informed that Siobhain had produced evidence of the crime, only that she had made the allegation of fraud. Joe was sure the original wills had all been destroyed, and if he could find Siobhain, he felt sure he could persuade her to withdraw the allegation.

Gossip was rife in the village; indeed, it seemed no-one could talk about anything else but this forthcoming trial. There had been a lot of speculation about the case in the local newspapers and even the national newspapers had given it a mention. Siobhain had made a deal with a daily newspaper to sell her story, after the trial ended, for a very large sum of money. She agreed to tell all about her involvement in this crime, and also about her ten-year romance with her boss Joe Maxwell.

Chapter 17

Apart from her son Lucas, his wife Lorna and her grandchildren, Eileen's only other close relatives in the village at the time of the infamous trial was a niece called Anna, the daughter of her late sister Rose Ann. Eileen, who married Tom Reilly in 1953, came from a large family. She tried to keep contact with them after the wedding but when Lucas was born she had little time for visiting. Her parents did not show much interest in their first grandson as they were preoccupied with their youngest son Sean, who was constantly in trouble – usually over drugs – and was in and out of prison. All three older brothers had difficulty getting work and left school as soon as it was legally allowed. With no qualifications or prospects they felt they had no future in Ireland and all three emigrated to Australia as soon as they reached eighteen. Her brother Sean, known as the black sheep of the family, often called round to see Eileen in the first year of her marriage whenever he needed money, and was even caught by Tom Reilly trying to burgle their home late one night. Needless to say Sean was then barred from visiting ever again and Eileen's parents were too embarrassed to call on Eileen again. When Sean turned eighteen he left home and went to Dublin, where he reassured his mother he would find work. He said he had some good friends there, most of whom were ex-convicts.

Eileen's two younger sisters were two very different personalities. The older of the two, Philomena, did visit Eileen whenever she could. They had always got along well. She adored Lucas and often babysat to let Tom and Eileen have an evening out together. When Philomena decide to emigrate, Eileen was devastated. In America, Philomena met a West Indian man and married him six months later. After a year she stopped writing to Eileen and she never returned to Ireland again.

Her younger sister Rose Ann remained at home and helped look after her parents when they became frail from old age. With the deaths of both parents, Rose Ann decided it was time she started enjoying herself. She developed a reputation for being a good time girl who had numerous affairs with married men. Eileen's mother used to say that Rose Ann and Sean were taking after her in-laws and were a real bad lot and of course the rest of her children were taking after her. Eileen's father believed his wife's bad health was all down to the worry inflicted on her by her children.

After ten years, Rose Ann Tierny decided to marry her on-and-off boyfriend, the village postman Declan Gilligan. He adored Rose Ann and turned a blind eye to the affairs she continued to have after they married. Rose Ann and Declan had one child, a girl called Anna, and the village gossips speculated as to who was the girl's real father.

The years passed by with no major mishaps until one night Rose Ann went out to meet her usual friends in the village pub. It was a birthday celebration, the music was good, and a lot of alcohol was consumed. At closing time

Rose Ann said goodbye to her friends and started walking unsteadily down a badly lit road. She then crossed the road a few yards from her home and was knocked down by a car driven recklessly by someone who failed to stop. She was killed instantly. The driver of the car was never apprehended.

Anna was a teenager at this time and she never got over the death of her mother. She remained at home, living with her father and never married. She developed a very hostile, aggressive manner, especially to anyone who tried to befriend her. Even at her mother's funeral she did not speak to her Aunt Eileen, seeming to resent everyone. At the time of the Finley/Maxwell scandal, Anna showed not only a great interest in the forthcoming trial but a certain delight that other people were going through difficult times.

Chapter 18

*H*arriet and Brian were now settled in their rented rooms in the village. Their son Sebastian continued to support them financially, since they had very little income. He was still living in their home in London and enjoying the great freedom of being able to bring his numerous girlfriends there without having to account to anyone. He was not the slightest bit concerned about his mother's neighbours and actually enjoyed seeing them peeping through their curtains. Sebastian had not been paying a lot of attention to his business since his wife had thrown him out. He was enjoying himself too much, spending more money than he had and too late he realised his business was in trouble.

Harriet was relaxing watching TV when the bombshell dropped. A letter from Sebastian informed his parents he could no longer look after them financially as his company had gone into liquidation. He told them he was not only broke with huge debts but was also worried about some of his creditors. Harriet did not want anyone to know about Sebastian's demise. It would be so embarrassing after all the bragging she had done about him, both in London and to the servants at Greenlawns (when she could get them to listen to her) during the holiday times she spent there. Her snobbery always over ruled everything else. She decided the solution to all their problems was to sell their house in London.

House prices in Ireland were still low at this time and with the profit from the house sale in London, the Finleys could live comfortably for some time. Sebastian would have to come to Ireland and live with them until Harriet decided her next course of action for him. She envisaged Sebastian starting up a new business in Ireland and with his intelligence and ability she knew it would happen quickly. Everything in the garden would be rosy again, providing the trial went in their favour, and she was confident she would not do prison time.

Everything went to plan. Sebastian secured a good deal on his parents' house in London, and arrived in the village in good spirits. In a relatively short period of time he managed to buy a three-bedroom house on the outskirts of the village, on behalf of his parents.

Harriet was feeling a lot more optimistic now and started going out with Brian and Sebastian to the village pub on Saturday nights to listen to Noel's band, although all three of them were ignored.

Chapter 19

*E*ileen's niece Anna Gilligan enjoyed causing trouble. Some people thought she needed mental health care, because she always seemed to be in the centre of every dispute around. She knew all the gossip about the Finleys and how they tried to swindle her aunt out of inheritance. She also heard about Sebastian and his wonderful wife and children in London. Meanwhile, Harriet also knew a few things about Anna from snooping on the servants at Greenlawns, and was secretly happy that Eileen had a dodgy relative.

Anna decided to go for a drink one Saturday night. She had no friends and usually caused an argument with anyone who sat beside her. She was intrigued to see the Finleys there, considering their predicament, but what really caught her eye was the middle-aged man with them. There was nothing special about this man, who was of medium height with a bald head and a beer belly. Anna sauntered over to the Finleys and introduced herself. Harriet's mouth dropped open. She couldn't believe the cheek of this person, but what else could you expect, given she was related to that conniving Eileen? She was about to tell her that her company was not welcome when Sebastian jumped up and introduced all of them, and invited Anna to join them for a drink.

So began the romance between Sebastian and Anna. They seemed instantly drawn towards each other. Anna was a good-looking woman whose only drawback was a psychopathic personality. She was tall, blonde and slim and dressed in the most outrageous styles she could get her hands on in charity shops. This brought her the attention she craved. When the Finleys left the pub that night Harriet was in a state of uncontrollable anger, and just when she thought things were getting better.

The Finley home was not a happy one from then on and all Harriet's powers of persuasion and manipulation seemed to fail her. Sebastian spent every spare minute with Anna and didn't show any inclination to look for a job. The lovebirds spent a lot of their time walking about the village aimlessly, holding hands and occasionally kissing, to the shock and horror of Harriet and the pointing fingers of half the villagers.

The Catholic Church in the village had a society called The Children of Mary. This organisation consisted of a number of Catholic women, whose function was to attend prayer meetings and do good works for the community. They had their special mass once a month, organised processions on various Church holidays and held a monthly meeting in the church hall to discuss progress and specific issues that needed attention. At their latest meeting one lady brought up a concern she felt was their duty to do something about and this turned out to be the adultery of Sebastian Finley. Being a small village where everybody knew everything about each other, it was common knowledge that Sebastian had a wife and two children in London and was now openly conducting an affair with Anna Gilligan.

A plan of action was decided upon and late one evening, the local parish priest, accompanied by four members of The Children of Mary paid a visit to the Finley home. Their aim was to persuade Sebastian Finley to end this relationship with Anna Gilligan and comply with the teachings of the Catholic Church. Harriet invited the group into her sitting room and offered them tea, as she thought it was some sort of welcoming committee. It was also a good opportunity to show off her expensive china tea service.

Before they had a chance to explain their mission or drink their tea, Sebastian and Anna walked in. They calmly announced, without waiting for introductions, that Anna was pregnant and they were both delighted. One of the women dropped and broke one of Harriet's precious china teacups, with the shock of what she just heard. She then ran out of the house followed by the rest of delegation.

To say this delegation was unsuccessful in its mission would be an understatement. Harriet and Brian never ventured into the village after that evening but shopped in the nearest town, some eight miles away, once a week. This was their only outing. Sebastian did not manage to start a new business and was oblivious to everything and everyone with the exception of Anna. He did not appear worried about the prospect of a new baby, despite having no job and with his money running out. Harriet felt her whole world was collapsing around her and she was powerless to do anything about it. Then the Finleys received notification that a trial date had been set.

Chapter 20

*I*n the year leading up to his trial, Joe Maxwell tried very hard to locate Siobhain. He knew if he had a chance to talk to her he could coach her into giving the most appropriate answers to the questions she would most certainly be asked. They might then have a chance of not going to prison. Barbara Maxwell had allowed him to remain in the family home because he had persuaded her that reports of a long-standing affair with Siobhain were grossly exaggerated and because he had worked closely with her she had become obsessed with him, even believed she was in love with him. Such feelings, he promised, were not reciprocated.

Jim Collins, Joe's father-in-law, knew all he needed to know about Joe's escapades over the years, and this fraud trial was the final straw. He deeply regretted allowing Joe into the family law firm and felt it had been a sorry day when Barbara had first laid eyes on him. He felt Barbara had more than her share of grief from her good-for-nothing husband throughout her married life and he knew she was always paying off his gambling debts. Even Barbara could not now afford a decent defence council for Joe and a public defender might be risky and not produce the desired outcome.

One Monday morning in April 2012, Jim Collins arranged a meeting with Joe Maxwell at a hotel outside the village, to discuss the trial. Joe did not get along well with his father-in-law, but at this point in time he needed all the help he could get. The deal Jim offered was the provision of the best legal counsel available in Ireland for his defence in his forthcoming trial, but on two conditions: that if the outcome of the court case was successful, Joe would leave Ireland and never see Barbara or their two sons again. Being a selfish man, Joe said he needed time to think about this proposal – after all, he loved his wife and sons and a sacrifice like this was too much to ask. Jim then offered to arrange a job for him in London, with a friend who ran an accountancy firm, after the trial ended and he was a free man. Joe still hesitated, so to sweeten the deal, Jim's final offer was two hundred thousand euros. Joe said he would give him an answer in a week. Both men shook hands with Jim thinking, 'He won't be able to resist this deal and how wonderful to have him out of my family's life for good'.

Joe thought about the deal very carefully and decided to take a gamble and turn it down. In his opinion, Barbara would come into a fortune when her father died, and with his age and health against him he might not have that long to wait. There was also the possibility of a big win on the horses, which he felt was more than due to him – and then Jim Collins could stick his deal.

In the betting shop the next day, Joe was discussing his predicament with his friend Eddy, who was manager of the shop. Eddy knew that Joe was good with figures and his shop needed someone to manage the books. He offered Joe a job with a reasonable salary plus two free bets a week, or two bets a week 'on the house', as he put it. This was too much for Joe to turn down. He decided to take the job and with the money he made he would hire a private detective to help him locate Siobhain. Who knows, he thought, he might win enough money to cover his own defence.

Joe, of course, told Barbara about her father's offer and this caused a huge row within the family. Barbara's mother tried to smooth things over, saying Jim was only thinking of what would be best for all and if Joe got a prison sentence, they would all need each other. Barbara was not swayed and did not speak to her parents for some time.

In the betting shop Joe was working hard and Eddy was also working hard watching Joe, as he knew what gambling addicts were like. Joe had his two free bets and numerous other bets on which most of his wages went, and still only won a few times. At the end of the first month, Joe owed a considerable amount to Eddy; in fact he was now working there for nothing and desperately trying to stick to the two free bets.

It was getting closer to the trial date and there was still no sign of Siobhain and Joe was beginning to panic. He heard a rumour that Siobhain was selling her story to a newspaper. He spent hours on the phone trying to speak to newspaper editors, with the hope of getting an address for Siobhain. The answers he got were mainly that they knew nothing about Siobhain, or they cited confidentiality.

Chapter 21

Siobhain had known she had to get away from the village as soon as she left the *garda* station on that fateful night when she reported the fraud, and got in touch with a friend from her past. When she first knew Michael Quinn he had just left university and had a great interest in investigative journalism. They had a few dates, although nothing serious came of it, but they remained friends. Apart from the occasional Christmas card they didn't really keep in touch. Last time Michael phoned her was just before she'd started working for Joe Maxwell. He was excited that he had landed the job of reporter for a local newspaper. She didn't expect he was still working there, as he was far too ambitious, but perhaps someone there might know of his whereabouts. As luck would have it, he was still working there but had progressed to the high office of editor.

When Siobhain finally got speaking to him, he was more than interested in her unusual story. He owned his own house in a big town called Poplea, about thirty-five miles from the village. He had not married and was not in a relationship. He invited Siobhain to his house immediately, so she packed her car with all her belongings and wrote a letter to the estate agent she rented her flat from. As she always paid a month's rent in advance she felt that was enough notice to give of her departure. She stated on her letter that she would not be returning. She put the letter with the keys to her flat through the estate agent's letterbox on her way out of the village of Prim.

When Siobhain had installed herself comfortably in Michael's house, she realised how lucky she had been, especially as Michael did not have any entanglements with anyone; in fact, he appeared to be devoid of friends and relatives. Siobhain told her story in great detail to Michael, leaving out nothing, from the time she met Joe Maxwell and became his mistress, to his gambling addiction and fraud perpetrated by both of them concerning wills, to the final conspiracy over Luke Mulryan. Thinking of some of the high profile names involved in this crime, Michael realised he was looking at a great scoop for his newspaper.

Michael invited Siobhain to stay at his house rent-free until the trial was over, and even afterwards if she desired, on condition that she would sell her story exclusively to his newspaper. He also promised her a considerable sum of money for the deal and said his newspaper would pay for a top barrister to represent her in court.

A few months later Michael discovered through the grapevine that Joe Maxwell was looking for Siobhain. Michael wanted to prevent their meeting at all costs, because he knew Siobhain was still in love with Joe. It could ruin everything for his plans for a major scoop, not to mention an idea he had for a book about this whole affair.

Michael told Siobhain he had a holiday cottage on the coast in County Donegal, where he spent whatever free time he could get. He thought it was a good idea that she should move there, as people at his office were beginning to gossip about him. It would also be easier and more enjoyable to write their story there. Siobhain loved everything about the cottage and the location but at times felt lonely, as Michael would only get up there a few times a month. He always locked his bedroom before going back to work, which intrigued Siobhain. Feeling bored one day Siobhain decided to pick the lock. She had a good nose around his room and was shocked when she opened his wardrobe. It was packed with designer dresses, skirts and jackets in every colour, and some very high-heeled designer shoes and sandals in size ten. There were also a half a dozen expensive blonde wigs. Siobhain sat down on his bed. It took her a few minutes to realise that Michael was a cross dresser. There was also a photograph of him in an elaborate frame with a group of male friends, all dressed in the latest high 'female' fashion with accessories. 'No wonder he hasn't got a girlfriend – the competition over clothes would probably be too much!' she thought. She locked the bedroom door carefully and pretended to know nothing about Michael's private life. She decided to keep it in mind, however, in case she ever needed to do a little blackmail after the trial was over, or maybe barter for more money for her story. Siobhain was a girl who always looked after number one.

When Siobhain told Michael she was thinking of going back to the village, as she was far too lonely with no friends stuck up there in Donegal, and at least there were some people there who still talked to her, he panicked and said he was going to New York on business the following week and would take her with him. She was not sure if he suspected she had been in his room or maybe just worried about losing her story. He told her she would love shopping there and maybe they could go together as he had a good eye for fashion. How true that was, she thought, and what fun it would be. After the New York trip, there were many other little treats, so life was not so lonely for Siobhain after all. Then she received notification of the trial date.

Chapter 22

*B*ack in the Finley residence Harriet was beginning to panic, and meeting with her public defence team did nothing to quell her anxieties. They continually reassured her, that as it was her first offence, she would probably get probation and/or a fine, and the same applied to Brian. They were both advised to plead guilty, as this would save time and money for the courts and could mean they'd be looked on more favourably. Harriet felt they should be looking at ways to discredit Joe Maxwell and his girlfriend Siobhain. After all, his gambling debts had started this whole terrible business, so the lawyers should be putting all the blame on them. When Harriet heard the rumour that Siobhain was selling her story to a newspaper that was engaging a top lawyer to defend her, she decided to persuade Brian to sell their house. It was the only way they would have enough funds for a decent defence. For once in his life Brian did not agree with his wife. He did not want to hand over the only security they had to a bunch of lawyers. They could end up with nothing, he said, and what would happen to Sebastian and Anna? It was bad enough they were both on the dole and expecting a baby, they could not become homeless as well.

Harriet argued that with a baby on the way, the couple would be eligible for a council house; 'such lovely houses in Ireland these days'. If they were homeless, this would hasten this whole process. Thinking about it, she felt quite sick. To have sunk from such a height socially to such low status made her feel faint. After a hot toddy she resumed her argument with Brian about selling, but to no avail.

The following week Harriet received a letter from her daughter-in-law Lucy, Sebastian's wife, saying she had been trying to get in touch with Sebastian for some time but all her efforts had failed. She wrote that as they were not legally separated, as far as she was concerned, they were still married and now she had decided to forgive him for his nasty behaviour and adultery.

Harriet welcomed the idea of Sebastian and Lucy getting back together again. The thought of seeing the back of that appalling Anna and her family connections really cheered her up. Her quest for the next few weeks was to work on Sebastian to make him see the error of his ways. This turned out to be another failure for Harriet. The result of all these arguments caused Anna's blood pressure to rise to the point when she was admitted to hospital as a precaution in her first pregnancy. Sebastian was furious with his mother and immediately contacted Lucy to demand a divorce.

Time seemed to be flying now and as it got nearer to the court date, Harriet got more anxious. Brian did not appear too worried. He believed Harriet could talk her way out of any situation and was smarter than most lawyers. When she started coaching him on the answers he should give, he began to have little niggles of doubt. The thought of going to prison at his time of life gave him the shivers. He would just have to keep faith in Harriet; after all, she had not let him down yet.

Chapter 23

Almost a year after their arrest at Dublin airport, Joe Maxwell and Brian and Harriet Finley arrived at the Central Criminal Court in Dublin, for the start of their trial. Siobhain was already there with her legal team. She avoided eye contact with them, especially with Joe. Their case had gathered a lot of public interest through local and national newspapers. Anything to do with injustice, like cheating charities out of much-needed money, by people who should know better, evoked outrage among many communities and even resulted in debates on TV and radio chat shows. A large crowd from the village travelled up to Dublin for the trial. Some came for the day bringing sandwiches and flasks of tea with them intending to enjoy the court 'entertainment', while others booked into hotels for a week. It was expected the trial would not last longer than a week, although crime trials are considered by the legal profession to be notoriously unpredictable.

The judge presiding over the trial was a man in his late fifties called James Hughes. He had a reputation for handing down harsh sentences for relatively minor offences and had no tolerance for anyone who had studied law committing a crime. Joe Maxwell was not a happy man when he discovered who would be judging his case.

The courtroom was packed with journalists from all over Ireland. There were also many relatives and acquaintances of the defendants there. In the front row of the gallery seats were Sebastian Finley and his girlfriend Anna; he thought it would be a fun day out for her, even though it was getting close to her time for giving birth. She felt entitled to be there as it was her aunt Eileen who had been defrauded. Sebastian made a great fuss of Anna by continually rubbing her back and drawing attention to her, as Harriet later described it. Noel and Eileen were not there as they were giving evidence later in the trial.

As this was a trial by jury, it took most of the morning to complete the court process. It was decided the first defendant to be called to the stand would be Joe Maxwell, and this would happen after lunch. This was a stressful time for all concerned and for Joe it seemed the longest hours of his life. He just wanted to get it over with, whatever the outcome.

Joe Maxwell took the stand at 2.30p.m., looking very uncomfortable, especially when he saw the scowling face of Judge Hughes. He was questioned for what seemed like hours about his involvement in changing wills, and in particular Luke's Mulryan's will. He was asked who instructed him to make any changes and what happened with regard to at least four charities who had not received expected legacies. He denied all charges against him, saying he had no money problems and would not stoop so low as to deprive charities of their entitlements. He stated that paranoid and obsessive people had a vendetta against him and he knew the truth would come out before the end of the trial.

The following morning was the turn of Brian Finley to take the stand. The prosecution team decided to leave Siobhain to be the last defendant called, as they regarded her as their trump card. Brian was feeling very shaky. He had not slept a wink the night before, worrying so much that even several brandies did not help. Now, to crown it all, he could not remember half of what Harriet had instructed him to say. He was questioned about his gambling and exactly who informed him of his inheritance. At this point he replied he was never bothered about money, it was easy come, easy go as far as he was concerned, and it was his wife who worried about money. On hearing this, Harriet fainted and had to be carried out of the courtroom. The trial was then adjourned until the following morning. Brian was now a broken man.

On day three of the trial, at 11a.m., Harriet Finley was called to the stand. At first she presented as a confident but hostile witness, answering every question with a question of her own. The judge had to intervene at least twice, instructing her to answer the question. She stated she had no memory of ever requesting Joe Maxwell to alter Luke's will, saying it was his suggestion as he had gambling debts. She stated he was under the influence of his secretary Siobhain, to whom he could never say no. She believed Siobhain was a greedy scheming woman who masterminded the entire deception and it had nothing to do with her or Brian. In the end, the prosecutor, who was very adept at his job, had her tied up in knots with his questions. She in turn didn't know who she blamed most. All she was certain of was that it was nothing to do with her and she did not want to go to prison.

Chapter 24

*T*he trial continued into the fourth day and Noel Finley was the next witness to be called. The first question asked by the prosecution lawyer was when precisely had Luke Mulryan informed him of his intention to leave him some of his inheritance. Noel said he didn't remember the exact date but thought it was around 1978, after Luke's racing business had become highly successful. He remembered it was at one of Luke's celebration parties. He explained Luke told him he was leaving half his estate to him, and the other half to Eileen Reilly. He also stated that Joe Maxwell, Luke's solicitor, had already drawn up this will.

The defence lawyer cross-examined Noel, asking first if Noel had been drinking at this party where he heard about his inheritance. Noel replied he had, but he was not drunk. He was then asked if he thought he was entitled to some inheritance in view of their long friendship, or if perhaps it was wishful thinking on his part. Noel was beginning to get annoyed with this tone of question and shouted he expected 'nothing from no one' and 'checking the authenticity of the solicitor's will should be enough for anyone'. There were no further questions.

Eileen Reilly was called to the stand in the afternoon

session. Eileen was very nervous and praying her past life with Luke Mulryan would not come into question. Her first question by the prosecution was how surprised was she to learn that Luke had wanted her to share in his substantial wealth. She replied that they had been friends from their youth and always got on well. She stated that after her husband's death, Luke had played a big part in her family's life. She was asked if there was any specific reason for leaving her half his estate. She replied that Luke had only two cousins – Noel and Brian Finley – and she understood he was leaving half his estate to Noel. In fact Joe Maxwell had informed her of this.

The defence lawyer appeared restrained in his questions to Eileen. Most of the questions were centred on the will and the inheritance. It was common knowledge among the villagers that Luke was Lucas Reilly's biological father, though no-one could be sure of what Lucas knew. Luke had kept his promise to Eileen never to divulge their secret, and Lucas had loved Tom Reilly as his father all his life. Both legal teams had somehow got knowledge of Lucas's birth, but it was not in the interest of the defence to bring this up in court as it would justify Luke leaving half his fortune to Eileen and strengthen the case for the prosecution. Eileen made a promise to herself to tell the whole truth to Lucas when the trial was over; she didn't want it to be made public knowledge before she had a chance to talk to Lucas. At 5 p.m. the defence lawyer said: 'No further questions'.

On Friday – the last day of the trial – Siobhain was called to the stand. She'd looked forward to this moment for so long and waited with bated breath for her chance to shine, to impress and dazzle her audience and think of all that lovely money she would make as a result. She was dressed in her favourite pale blue suit and matching accessories and was especially pleased with her hairdresser, who had given such shine to her flowing curly locks. In fact she looked more like an actress auditioning for a part in a play than a defendant in a fraud case. Before taking the oath, she gave Judge Hughes her most brilliant smile and for a fleeting moment he almost smiled back. The first question from the barrister was: 'Please explain to the court how you became involved with the other defendants in this crime of fraud'. Siobhain started from the beginning, a long, drawn-out account of her first meeting with Joe Maxwell. She described how their love affair began two years before she started working in his law firm, she stated it was love at first sight for both of them, and how, over the next ten years Joe had spent more time with her than with his family. She said she became aware of Joe's love for gambling on the horses early in their relationship, but when he lost heavily in those early years he didn't seem to have any difficulty in paying his debts. Siobhain's barrister tried to hurry her along and get to the main part of the question but Siobhain was having no part of this. She was determined to tell her entire story with emphasis on her sex life. Michael Quinn, her newspaper editor friend had pointed out to her that the more she could spice up an account of her sex life, the more money they could both make from newspaper sales and the book he would eventually write. He told her he could make her a celebrity, and how much she would enjoy the fame and the money.

Siobhain talked about Joe's tattoo – a rabbit on his left buttock which he had acquired during his wild days at university. She said it became a code for sex between them and whenever one of them sang 'Run Rabbit, Run' it meant they were in the mood for bedroom antics.

Barbara Maxwell sat in court with her head down, cringing with embarrassment at all these disgusting revelations about her husband. What a fool she had been to believe Joe. She had no doubt now about his affair with Siobhain; how else would she have known about his rabbit tattoo? The courtroom was abuzz with laughing and talking and journalists running out to get their stories in their evening editions. Judge Hughes threatened to remove everyone from the court if order was not restored.

Siobhain continued with accounts of romantic holidays and weekends away with Joe and how she only realised he was having financial problems when he stopped buying her presents. She said that by now she was totally under his spell, and would have done anything he asked. It was his idea to alter the wills of people with no relatives. He reassured her that no-one would lose by doing this, and she'd believed him. Joe drew up new wills for elderly people who had died leaving their estates to various charities, only now the charity was Joe Maxwell. She said Joe had asked her to be the witness to these transactions. When asked how many wills were altered, she answered 'five' but stated she had destroyed only four original wills by burning them. The only one she had not got round to destroying was that of Luke Mulryan. Luke's original will and the forged will were then produced for the court.

The defence lawyers asked Siobhain why she had gone to the authorities with her evidence of fraud, knowing that she was involved and could be prosecuted. She replied she was devastated by Joe's betrayal after all she had done for him over the years, things no other woman would stoop so low to do, and he had given her his solemn promise of marriage – which he had no intention of keeping. She also said that changing Luke Mulryan's will was at the request and insistence of Brian and Harriet Finley, and it happened at a time when Joe had lost heavily on the horses. The defence lawyers said Siobhain's evidence was that of a woman scorned and could not be relied upon. They also put it to her that she was implicating the Finleys because they had not wanted her with them on their holiday to the Bahamas. In the end, the evidence of the forged and original wills placed before the court was irrefutable.

The jury took a short time to deliberate and deliver the verdict of guilty to all four defendants. It was late on a Friday afternoon but Judge Hughes gave a lengthy lecture to the four people in the dock. He called them all equally greedy, immoral and without conscience. He said they showed not an ounce of remorse for their crime. He singled out Joe Maxwell as the worst offender of all, not just because of his horrendous crime but for bringing The Law Society into disrepute. He stated it took the participation of all four defendants to carry out this deception, and it was their lavish celebration of getting away with breaking the law that resulted in their apprehension. Joe Maxwell was sentenced to eight years imprisonment. He was also struck off for life by The Law Society. His sentence was harsh, because – as the Judge put it – he was an officer of the law and was aware how serious his crime and its consequences were. Brian and Harriet Finley were both sentenced to five years imprisonment. The judge said it would have been longer had it not been for the fact it was their first offence. On hearing this Harriet had another fainting spell and had to be carried outside, with Brian shouting to her, 'We will only have to do half that time'.

Siobhain received two years' probation because she had co-operated and become witness for the prosecution. The judge stated that without her coming forward this crime might never have come to light. She couldn't wait to get outside the court, where she talked recklessly with reporters. She even ventured to tell them she thought the judge fancied her. Eventually her friend Michael Quinn dragged her away. She so enjoyed the limelight.

Chapter 25

*N*oel drove Eileen back to the village of Prim from Dublin. She had stayed with a friend who lived near the court building. Noel had stayed in a small hotel for the week of the trial. On their journey home while discussing the trial and its outcome at some length, Eileen told Noel the most urgent thing on her mind now was telling Lucas the true story of his birth and that his biological father was Luke. She had spent the whole week worrying that this secret would come out during the trial, especially when Harriet took the stand. She was well aware that Harriet never liked her; in fact, Luke used to joke with her about it and say how vindictive Harriet was.

Noel agreed it was important to put the record straight tonight, as you could never tell what Siobhain had been saying to the newspapers. He reassured Eileen that it would all turn out OK and he knew she could rely on Lucas's wife Lorna to be supportive. He dropped Eileen at her house and declined an invitation to some tea or refreshments. She could feel her heart pounding as she walked up to the door. Before she had a chance to put her key in the lock, the door opened and out bounced her two grandsons. It was Friday night and the twins were all dressed up for a party night with their mates. They kissed their grandmother, saying they were looking forward to hearing all about the trial next day and with a wave they were gone.

Lucas and Lorna were just finishing dinner and were delighted to see Eileen home safely. Eileen's first words were: 'I have something important to talk to you about, Lucas.' Lorna excused herself, saying she had reports to complete for work.

Eileen then said to her son that she fancied a small whiskey; she needed all the help she could get. She had not got very far with the story of his birth when Lucas put his arms around her. 'Stop worrying,' he said. 'I have known all about this for a very long time.' He told his mother that Lorna helped him get a DNA test when she was pregnant with the twins as she believed medical history to be important. They had both heard all the rumours and village gossip. Working in the local hospital, Lorna had no problem getting Luke Mulryan and Tom Reilly's blood groups for comparison. The DNA result proved conclusively that Luke was his father. He told her he could not have wished for a better father than Tom Reilly and had loved him all his life. They only thing he regretted was not being able to tell his boys that Luke Mulryan was their grandfather. At this point Eileen cried, saying she had also wished for this. Eileen went on to explain to Lucas that in the Fifties, unmarried mothers usually went into convents where the nuns removed their babies for adoption or sale soon after birth. She was so lucky to have Tom Reilly, who really loved her, and in time she had loved him in return. She told him their lives together had been very happy. She also told him about her time with Luke Mulryan and how she had not informed him about the pregnancy, believing mistakenly he no longer loved her. She said a little about his mother and Lucas replied, 'Some grandmother she would have been.'

Eileen replied she might have been great as a grandmother, feeling a great weight have been lifted from her shoulders. Lucas said that he had told Lorna the whole story, as he had no secrets from her. He also told her that Lorna and he would tell the twins, as you never knew what kind of stories would turn up in the newspapers following the trial. Once again he reassured her that the twins were modern, well-adjusted young men who would not have any problem with this revelation.

Chapter 26

*M*any of the national newspapers carried the story of the trial the following day but the tabloids had a field day with photographs, mostly of Siobhain, and cartoons of Joe Maxwell depicting him as a rabbit. One paper had a four-page spread of the love affair between Siobhain and Joe. Another tabloid presented Siobhain's story in a series of instalments. Michael Quinn's newspaper was supposed to have the exclusive but carried little more detail of Siobhain's own story than the other papers. It appeared that Siobhain had sold her story to anyone who would pay on the steps of the courthouse after the trial was over.

Michael Quinn was furious and only paid her fifty thousand euros, which was a quarter of what he had promised. He would not have paid her anything if it was not for the possibility that she might have found out about his cross-dressing. She seemed happy with the money after he pointed out she had broken their agreement. She was, however, invited onto two radio shows and one late night TV chat show. One tabloid invited her to be an agony aunt in a teenage section of their paper, although this particular job only lasted a week as some of the advice she offered almost caused the newspaper to be sued.

With no job prospects in the legal secretary business, Siobhain decided to invest the money she'd made selling her story. She bought a house with a flower shop attached on the outskirts of Dublin. It was on a busy road *en route* to the west of Ireland. She thought it was good investment. To cover all her options she joined an exclusive dating agency, with the same ambition she'd always had: to marry a rich man.

Joe Maxwell's family never forgave him for the hurt he had caused and the great wrong he had done. Barbara Maxwell started divorce proceeding immediately after Siobhain's revelation in court. Her parents were pleased about this and asked her to go and live near them in Westport, County Mayo, where Jim Collins had his retirement home. After a family conference, Barbara's sons said how relieved they were to finally get away from the village and told of the annoyance and harassment they had endured since the trial. Barbara, on hearing this, put her house on the market and before the sale was completed she moved with her sons to her parents' house in County Mayo. She would buy a place of her own in the future, but for now she couldn't bear to stay in the village a minute longer.

A few weeks after the trial, Anna gave birth to a baby girl. It seemed Sebastian always produced girls and there was no son to carry on the wonderful Finley name, which was always a sore point with Sebastian. They decided to have their baby baptised and throw a celebration party. Anna enjoyed having his parents' house to herself and thought how well it had all worked out. The icing on the cake was the long sentence Brian and Harriet received. No longer did she have to endure the criticism and insults she'd had constantly from Harriet, and she was equally happy that Harriet didn't want her to visit her in prison. However, Sebastian had applied for a visitor's pass to each prison for his partner and the baby, saying his parents were anxious to see their new grandchild.

The first visit by Sebastian, Anna and baby to the women's prison did not go well. Apart from the baby crying for an hour, Anna was dressed in an 'outrageous hippy-style outfit' that embarrassed Harriet. Even in prison her snobbery had not diminished and she had told stories to the other inmates of her wonderful family with their great jobs and wonderful prospects. She whispered to Sebastian not to bring Anna again. As they left the prison visiting room, another visitor called out: 'Anna Gilligan, is it really you?' to the shock and horror of Harriet. She couldn't believe that someone else in this awful place could know her son's girlfriend.

Sebastian thought it was such an inconvenience having to visit two different prisons and the time he spent travelling there was awful. He said to Anna: 'They are so behind the times here, they should have prisons for couples'.

Sebastian and Anna got a shock when they visited the parish priest to arrange the baptism service. It was the same priest who had visited Harriet's home with a view to ending Sebastian's adultery and he now refused point blank to perform the ceremony. Sebastian was so angry he wanted to shake the priest and said something he thought would really annoy him: 'I will have our daughter baptised in the Protestant church and bring her up a Protestant'.

On his next visit to his mother, Sebastian asked if he could sell her house, as he wanted to return to London.

He promised they could all live together again when they got out of prison and he knew his mother wanted to go back to England. Harriet would not even consider this proposal. She knew how it would all end and anyway she didn't want anything to do with Anna when they returned to London. She told Sebastian to get an estate agent to rent the house as soon as they were ready to leave. She was so disappointed in her son… to think she'd had such high hopes for him.

Harriet was now spending all the time she was allowed in the prison library, reading law books. She planned to conduct her own and Brian's appeal against their sentences. She believed the public defender was useless and the cause of their guilty verdict and she could have done a better job herself. She was beginning to feel less depressed now and the money she would get from renting the house would be a nice little nest egg for them on their release.

Sebastian, however, arranged for the estate agent to let the house and send the monthly rent to his address in London as soon as he found a base. Within a week he was safely installed in a flat in London with Anna and baby daughter. He stated how wonderful it would be to be near his daughters again and his grandchildren; after all, he was a family man. Harriet and Brian had no idea about his deception over their house.

Brian became resigned to his fate and was determined to be as polite as possible to everyone 'inside'. No longer could he afford to bully other people as he did in the construction business. He managed to become friends with inmates who also had the gambling bug. This small group of prisoners spent all their time betting with cigarettes and pennies on anything that moved, from creepy crawlies to the timekeeping of the staff. They also played cards where the winners got the biggest or the best portions of food. Prison was not as bad as he'd expected, thought Brian.

Chapter 27

*L*uke's will was finally legally and properly administered. The dilemma for Eileen and Noel, who had both been left equal shares in the huge estate, was what to do with it. Noel had stayed so long in the village because he loved music and his *ceili* band still had regular gigs in the local pub. So Noel asked Eileen if she would consider marrying him as it would simplify so many things, and they had always got on so well together. Eileen replied that she was too old and set in her ways and she only ever had one love in her life.

After many weeks of discussions and debates with Eileen's family and Noel, a solution was found. It was decided Noel and Eileen would sell their respective houses and convert Greenlawns into four large apartments. The twins were now in their twenties and qualified vets like their father. They worked in the family business and were a great asset to Lucas, who was now in control of running Greenlawns and its many companies. He had a large staff, which was necessary with the racing stables and stud farm. Lorna had given up her job in the hospital and was very busy as company secretary.

The living arrangements worked out well for all. They all remained close to each other while still maintaining their own private space. The house still had a ballroom and a large games room in the basement, which greatly appealed to the twins and their friends, when they were not involved in horse show jumping. Show jumping was a passion with the twins and their dream was realised through the life and efforts of their grandfather Luke Mulryan, as Eileen and Noel often remarked.

On the anniversary of Luke's death, a celebration of his life was held at Greenlawns in the newly renovated ballroom. The whole village was invited. One speech, which was more memorable than others, was made by Lucas. 'Raise your glasses to the memory of my father Luke Mulryan, and also to my mother Eileen and cousin Noel Finley... the rightful NEXT OF KIN (N.O.K.).'